To
Carter,

MERRY CHRISTMAS

Love from,

....

'Twas the night before Christmas,
when all through the house,
Not a creature was stirring,
not even a mouse;

Carter's stocking was hung
by the chimney with care,
In hope that St. Nicholas
soon would be there.

Carter was nestled all snug in his bed,
While visions of candy canes danced in his head.
And Mom in her kerchief, and Dad in his cap,
Had just settled down for a long winter's nap.

0 0 1

sleep~~s~~ until
santa visits

When out on the street
there arose such a clatter,
Carter sprang from his bed
to see what was the matter.

Away to the window
Carter flew like a flash,
Tore open the curtains,
threw open the latch.

Santa
PLEASE
STOP
HERE!

Love,
CARTER

The moon on the blanket
of new-fallen snow,
Shone bright as midday
on the objects below—

When, what to Carter's
wondering eyes should appear,
But a miniature sleigh
and eight tiny reindeer.

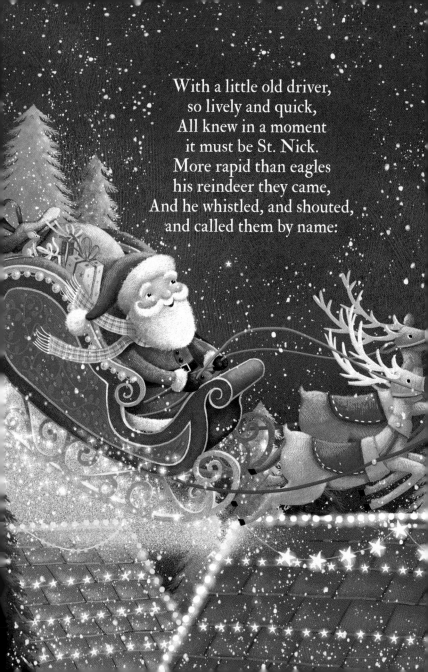

With a little old driver,
so lively and quick,
All knew in a moment
it must be St. Nick.
More rapid than eagles
his reindeer they came,
And he whistled, and shouted,
and called them by name:

"Now, Dasher! Now, Dancer!
Now, Prancer and Vixen!
On, Comet! On, Cupid!
On, Donder and Blitzen!
Take me to Carter's chimney;
follow my call!
Now dash away, dash away,
dash away all!"

And then, in a twinkling,
Carter heard on the roof
The prancing and pawing
of each little hoof.

As Carter pulled in his head
and was turning around,
Down the chimney
St. Nicholas came with a bound.

He was dressed all in fur,
from his head to his foot,
And his clothes were all tarnished
with ashes and soot.
A bundle of toys he had
flung on his back,
And he looked like a peddler
holding his pack.

BLESS
OUR
HOME

His eyes–how they twinkled!
His dimples–how merry!
His cheeks were like roses,
his nose like a cherry.
His droll little mouth
was drawn up like a bow,
And the beard on his chin was
as white as the snow.

Dear Santa,
Welcome to
my house!
I hope you enjoy the
yummy treats I have
left out for you.
Love from your
biggest fan,

Carter
xxx

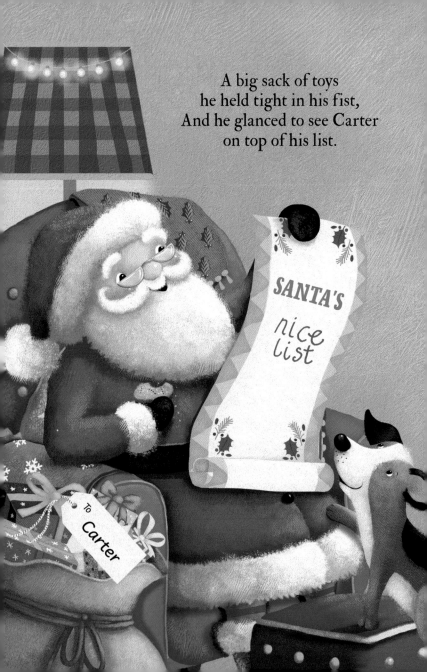

A big sack of toys
he held tight in his fist,
And he glanced to see Carter
on top of his list.

SANTA'S
nice
list

To
Carter

He had a broad face
and a little round belly
That shook when he laughed,
like a bowl full of jelly.

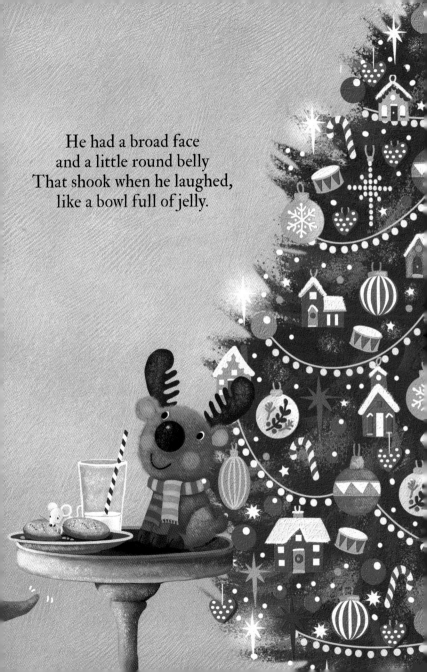

He was chubby and plump,
a right jolly old elf,
And Carter laughed when he saw him,
in spite of himself.

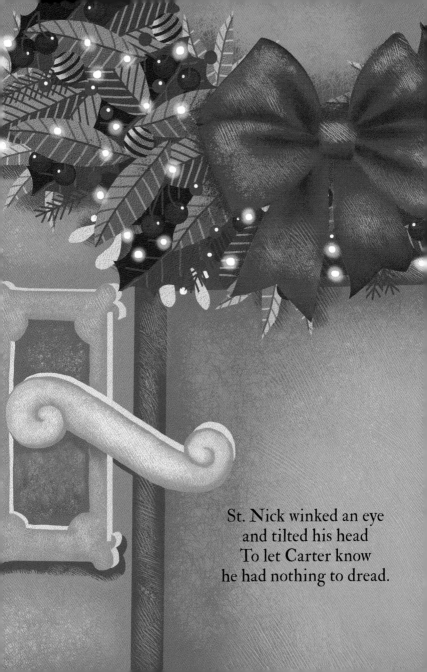

St. Nick winked an eye
and tilted his head
To let Carter know
he had nothing to dread.

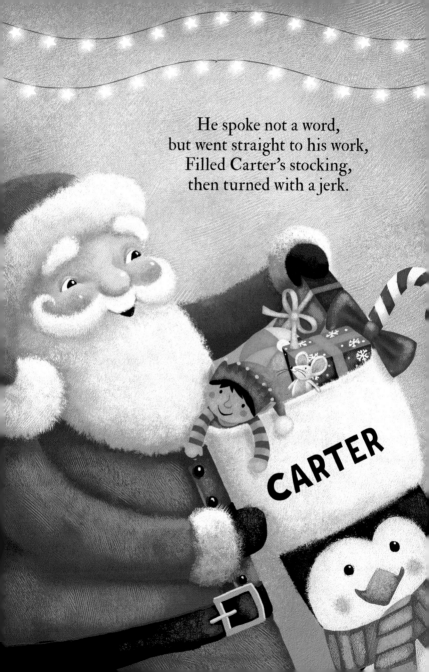

He spoke not a word,
but went straight to his work,
Filled Carter's stocking,
then turned with a jerk.

And tapping his finger
at the side of his nose,
And giving a nod,
up the chimney he rose.

He sprang to his sleigh,
to his team gave a whistle,
And away they all flew
like the down of a thistle.
But St. Nicholas exclaimed,
as he drove out of sight–

THANK
YOU
Santa

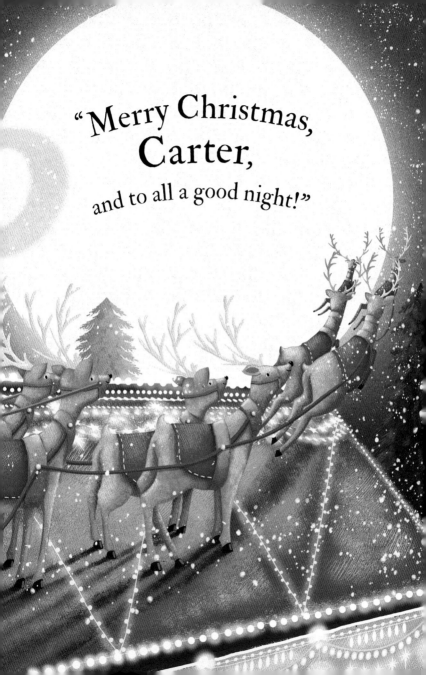

"Merry Christmas, Carter, and to all a good night!"

My Christmas Wishes

Carter, can you color in Santa?

To Carter

Adapted from the poem by Clement C. Moore
Illustrated by Jo Parry
Designed by Ryan Dunn and Nicky Scott

Published by Put Me In The Story,
a publication of Sourcebooks.
P.O. Box 4410, Naperville, Illinois 60567-4410
(630) 536-1104
sourcebookskids.com

Date of Production: May 2024
Run Number: 5039043
Printed and Bound in China (GD)
10 9 8 7 6 5 4 3 2 1

MIX
Paper | Supporting
responsible forestry
FSC® C117745
FSC
www.fsc.org

put me
in the
story®
Bestselling books starring your child!